Fickle Fiona

Written by Kate Hanscom

Illustrations by Lynda Hanscom

Fickle Fiona

ISBN: 978-1-62020-227-2
eISBN: 978-1-62020-325-5

Illustrations: Lynda Hanscom
Cover design and typesetting: Matthew Mulder
E-book conversion: Anna Riebe

AMBASSADOR INTERNATIONAL
Emerald House
427 Wade Hampton Blvd.
Greenville, SC 29609, USA
www.ambassador-international.com

AMBASSADOR BOOKS
The Mount
2 Woodstock Link
Belfast, BT6 8DD, Northern Ireland, UK
www.ambassador-international.com

The colophon is a trademark of Ambassador

Manufactured by Color House Graphics, Inc.
Grand Rapids, MI, USA
September 2013
Job# 40946

For Ma, Dad, Danny and John

— Kate

For my parents, Sam and Leda

— Lynda

We are so grateful for the unwavering love and support of our family and friends.

Your belief in us has pushed us to dig deeper and be better.

Thank you!

Danny stuck his head into his little sister's room. "Fiona, what's taking you so long? We want to go to the park!"

"Yeah, Fiona! Hurry up and change out of your pajamas!" John chimed in.

"I'll be ready … as soon as I decide what to wear." Fiona turned toward her dresser full of clothes.

Her brothers tapped their feet, shook their heads, and waited. Fiona stared at her open drawers, hemming and hawing, thinking and pondering, mulling and stewing over her decision. She simply could not decide what to wear!

"Fickle Fiona Joyce! You can never make a choice! Here, let me help you!" Danny stepped in and pulled a pink and blue polka-dotted shirt from the drawer.

"And here! Throw these on!" John added, handing her a pair of green and orange striped pants.

Fiona looked at her outfit in the mirror. Her blue eyes grew as big as two beach balls. "Oh my goodness! Polka dots and stripes! I look like a circus clown!" She sighed and shrugged. "But I suppose this is better than wearing pajamas."

After breakfast, the kids scurried to the toy box to choose toys to bring to the park. Danny quickly reached for the soccer ball. He loved to bounce it off his head. John picked the baseball and mitt. He liked to imagine that he was the pitcher for his favorite baseball team.

"What are you going to bring with you?" Mom asked Fiona, watching her eye the pink jump rope, the sidewalk chalk, and the stuffed black bear.

"Hmmm … what should I bring?" Fiona hemmed and hawed, thought and pondered, mulled and stewed as she tried to decide.

"My sweet girl, Fickle Fiona Joyce! You can never ever make a choice! I will choose something for you."

Mom randomly reached into the toy box and grabbed … Buddy's chew toy!

"WHOOOOEEEE!!! YUCK!" Fiona yelped as sticky, stinky slobber dripped from the squeaky toy. "Well, it's better than nothing!" she told herself and joined her family in the car.

At the park, Danny and John sprinted like cheetahs to the open field to play. Dad followed closely behind them, but Fickle Fiona didn't know which direction to look in first!

"Why don't we play on the jungle gym? That looks like fun!" Mom suggested.

"Sure!" Fiona's eyes lit up like delightful fireflies.

The jungle gym had a big red twirly slide, bright blue monkey bars, and three green swings that looked as if you could reach the sky if you swung high enough. With a skip in her step, Fiona grabbed Mom's hand and headed that way.

"Hmmm … swings, slide, or monkey bars?" Fiona hemmed and hawed, thought and pondered, mulled and stewed after she reached the jungle gym. She looked back and forth and back and forth until playful children filled the entire space! Soon all that was left were the baby bouncers!

"This is silly! I am much too tall for this!" Fiona shrugged and chuckled, but she supposed that the horse on a spring was better than nothing at all. So she crammed her long legs on the tiny toy.

Soon the pleasant melody of the ice cream truck filled the air. As the bells got closer, Danny and John scurried over like excited puppies.

"Mom! Mom! May we get an ice cream?" Danny asked.

"Please? Pretty please?!?" John pleaded. Fiona fervently nodded at the fabulous idea.

"Well, this is our special day out. I suppose a sweet treat would be fine," Mom said.

Dad smiled, reached into his pocket, and pulled out a few dollars.

"Thank you!" they all shouted. They ran to stand behind a growing line of antsy and excited children.

"Wait one second, Fiona." Mom crouched down to speak face to face. "There are a lot of kids and only one ice cream truck. If you are too fickle, the ice cream man may run out of your choice!"

Fiona did not heed her mother's warning. Instead, she stood to the side of the line and eyeballed the tempting pictures of ice cream. More and more children filed in front of her as she hemmed and hawed, thought and pondered, mulled and stewed over her choices. At last, she decided on the fudge pop and jumped in line.

"May I please have a fudge pop, sir?" she asked when it was finally her turn.

"Oh, I'm so sorry, little girl. That boy got the last one. I do have frog's face ice creams with delicious gumball noses!" He held up a green ice cream to show Fiona.

"EEEK!!!" Fiona shrieked and sputtered and squirmed.

"Frog ice cream will give me frog warts!"

She ran back to her parents and threw her hands in the air. "That's it! I am through being Fickle Fiona!" she exclaimed. "I just couldn't make a decision! Now, my outfit doesn't match. I brought Buddy's dog toy to the park. I never got a turn on the monkey bars, and worst of all … I missed out on ICE CREAM!" From the corner of her eye, she saw chocolate ice cream drip down a little boy's chin. "From now on, I am going to make up my mind more quickly!"

Just as she finished speaking, her brothers ran up. "Mom and Dad, thank you for the scrumptious ice cream! What should we do next?"

"I have a suggestion!" Fiona said, raising her pointer finger as high as the sky.

"You do?" Danny looked confused. "You are usually so fickle!"

"Well, I thought we might play a family game of kickball!" she exclaimed. "Dad, you can be the pitcher. Mom, would you be the catcher? Danny, how about centerfield? John, would you be the kicker? I will take first base."

"Awesome! We love kickball!" Danny and John high-fived each other.

"What a wonderful idea, Fiona!" Mom said as Dad proudly patted Fiona's back.

As the family headed over to the field, Fiona thought aloud. "Now that I'm not fickle anymore, I may need a new nickname. Feisty Fiona … or maybe Fancy Fiona … or better yet, Funny Fiona!"

Mom and Dad flashed Fiona a look. She blushed.

"On second thought, I think I'll be happy just being me."

What Is a Simile?

A simile [SIH-muh-lee] is a figure of speech in which different things are compared by the use of the words *like* or *as* (simile, Merriam-Webster Dictionary). Similes can be great tools that a writer may use to add description and emphasis to their stories.

Look below to see how similes make each sentence more vibrant and descriptive.

Allie is sweet.

Allie is as sweet as sugar!

My brother is strong.

My brother is as strong as an ox!

I slept well last night.

I slept like a log last night!

Now, can you go back and find the similes in *Fickle Fiona*?

1) Her blue eyes grew as big as two beach balls.

2) I look like a circus clown!

3) At the park, Danny and John sprinted like cheetahs to the open field to play.

4) "Sure!" Fiona's eyes lit up like delightful fireflies.

5) As the bells got closer, Danny and John scurried over like excited puppies.

6) "I have a suggestion!" Fiona said, raising her pointer finger as high as the sky.

About the Author

Kate Hanscom grew up as the youngest of three children in Utica, New York. A graduate of Stonehill College, she currently lives in Auburn, Massachusetts, with her family.

Since the publication of her first book, *Literal Lily*, Kate has found joy and fulfillment in sharing her stories with those who will learn from and be delighted by the story most—children! In her sophomore book, *Fickle Fiona*, she hopes that children will be equally entertained and challenged to expand their minds, imaginations, and vocabulary!

Writing has been a creative outlet for Kate since childhood. She loves dreaming up new characters and watching in awe as they come to life. She hopes that when readers meet Fiona, they are encouraged to laugh, learn, and not let their own indecision get in the way of whatever it is that they want to do!

About the Illustrator

Lynda Hanscom is originally from Long Island, New York. She holds a BFA from St. John's University and an MAT from the Rhode Island School of Design. As an art teacher, she guided hundreds of budding student artists from kindergarten through high school to be creative through drawing, painting, and sculpting.

In this, her third book, Lynda has enjoyed bringing the words of *Fickle Fiona* to life. Also the illustrator for *Tough Tommy* (a children's bereavement book) and *Literal Lily*, Lynda lives in Northern Connecticut with her loving and supportive husband, Doug, and draws constant joy and inspiration from her family.

For more information about

KATE HANSCOM

&

FICKLE FIONA
please visit:

www.katehanscom.com
www.facebook.com/katehanscomauthor

. . . .

For more information about
AMBASSADOR INTERNATIONAL
please visit:

www.ambassador-international.com
@AmbassadorIntl
www.facebook.com/AmbassadorIntl